Teachers Explain It All™

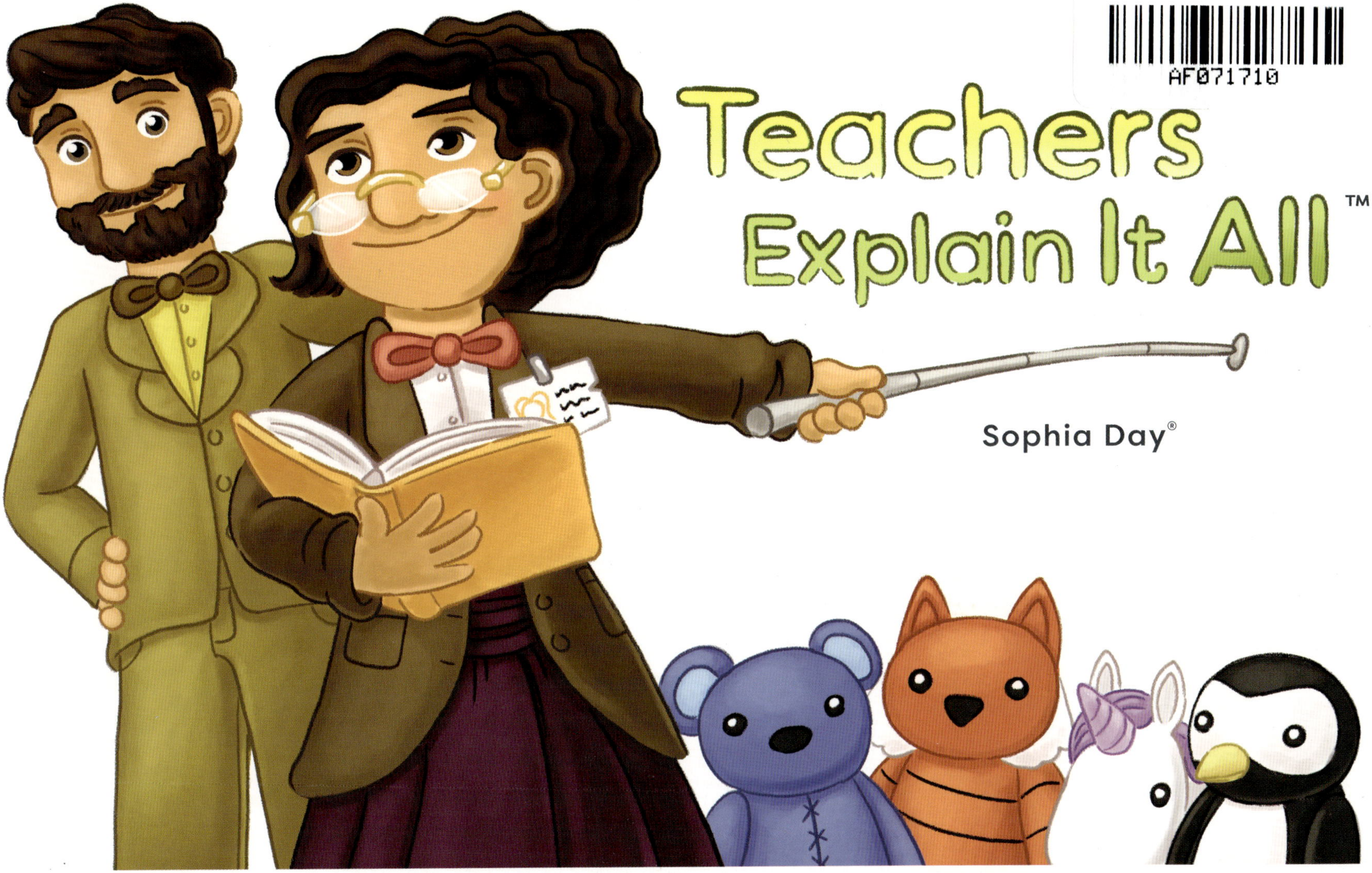

Sophia Day®

Written by Megan Johnson   Illustrated by Timothy Zowada

The Sophia Day® Creative Team-
Megan Johnson, Timothy Zowada, Stephanie Strouse,
Kayla Pearson, Celestte Dills, Patty Lopez Gregersen, Mel Sauder

A **special thank you** to our team of reviewers who graciously give us feedback, edits, and help ensure that our products remain accurate, applicable, and genuinely diverse.

Text and pictures copyrighted © 2021 by MVP Kids Media, LLC.

All rights reserved. No part of this publication may be reproduced in whole or in part by any mechanical, photographic, or electronic process, or in the form of any audio or video recording, nor may it be stored in a retrieval system or transmitted in any form or by any means now known or hereafter invented or otherwise copied for public or private use without the written permission of MVP Kids Media, LLC.

Published and distributed by
MVP Kids Media, LLC - Mesa, Arizona, USA.
Made in China.

Designed by Stephanie Strouse

ISBN 978-1-64786-262-6
DOM Jan 2021
Job #16-002-01

Hi! I'm Miriam. Someday, I want to be a teacher.

Smiles are the only thing I want to spread, so I will wash my hands A LOT!

science . . .

and more!

I will get creative to make sure everyone can be involved.

I'll record my students' learning and progress.

We'll go on meaningful field trips.

I will watch out for **bullying** and help students care for one another.

I'll probably teach classes online, too. I can teach students how to use their computers.

A **teacher's** job never ends.

. . . if I can find the answer . . .

An interview with a REAL Teacher!

CAROL HOLMOND
2nd Grade Teacher

Q: When did you know you wanted to become a teacher?

A: I've always liked teaching. I am a retired Sheriff Deputy and had been sent on occasion to speak to college classes or other groups about what I did with the Sheriff's Department. Then, in 2007, I learned that there was a school in dire need of a 2nd grade teacher. I was retired by then, I had a bachelor's degree in English, and I was asked to teach second graders at a private school. I loved the children and became instantly invested in their progress. I am now beginning my fourteenth year. The rewards are countless and range from seeing their eyes light up when they've met a goal, to watching them walk across the stage at graduation. There's nothing like it.

Q: What degree or qualifications are required to become a teacher?

A: Most schools require a bachelor's degree in education and a teaching certificate; however, some charter and private schools may have different requirements or teaching needs. There are legal credentials the government requires such as fingerprint cards and background checks, but each school usually keeps track of those to make sure they're in order.

Q: What character traits are most important for a teacher to develop?

A: A very important trait for a teacher to develop is organization. Other important traits are patience, kindness, understanding, and flexibility. Each student comes with his or her own personality. An effective teacher is aware that children learn in different ways and should be willing to adjust and address each child's needs.

Q: What habits have you made successful?

A: One habit I've developed quite successfully is record keeping. It is important to be able to keep an accurate record of grades, classroom behavior, class participation, students' classroom obligations, and the many more details that affect the class. This type of logging gives me a perspective of character and habits that students are developing.

Q: What is your favorite part of your job?

A: The favorite part of my job is seeing that spark of clarity in the eyes of a student when grasping a new concept—when a math procedure all of a sudden makes sense, or a reluctance to read aloud turns into an eagerness to read aloud because the skill has sharpened with practice. I live for those moments.

Q: What are some of the challenges in your work?

A: Probably the most frequent challenge is staying on time. There don't seem to be enough hours in a day, and before you know it, it's time to wrap things up to either go on to the next subject or prepare to leave for the day.

Q: What do you want future teachers to know?

A: I want future teachers to know that teaching is one of the most gratifying professions a person can choose. There is something about watching a child grow and learn, meet challenges and goals, and then walk across the stage to accept their diploma, and knowing you had a part in their accomplishment.

Meet the
mvpkids
featured in
Teachers Explain It All™
and their family

Miriam Nasser

Miriam loves reading books and making up her own stories to tell to others. She asks a lot of questions, and once she knows an answer, she can't help but tell others about it. She enjoys helping younger children, and her dad says she'd make a great teacher someday. He should know—he's a college professor!

Dr. Abdul Nasser
Father

Mrs. Salma Nasser
Mother

Sara Nasser
Sister

Adam Nasser
Brother

Reema Nasser
Grandmother

Mohammed Bassara
Grandfather

Sara Bassara
Grandmother

Julia Rojas
MVP Kid

Sarah Cohen-Goldstein
MVP Kid

Yong Chen
MVP Kid

Grow up with our MVPkids.

CELEBRATE!™ SERIES

Board Books

Ages 0-6

Paperbacks

Ages 4-8

help me BECOME™
Early Elementary
Ages 4-10

I Can Be an MVP!
Ages 2-6

help me UNDERSTAND™
Elementary
Ages 6-12

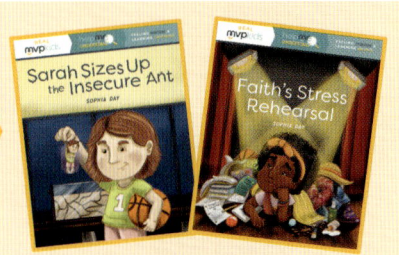

MIGHTY TOKENS — READ TOGETHER
Ages 4-8

DNA CHRONICLES™
Ages 8 and up

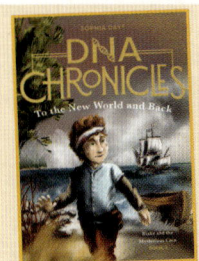

Playful Apprentice™
Ages 4-10

SOPHIA DAY'S® instill SEL® Instill Character®

Learn more about our books, puppets, classroom and home SEL programs, apps, and more at www.MVPKids.com.